The Songbird Army

by

Julia Blackburn

ROOT
BRANCH

Root & Branch Publishing

First published in Great Britain in 2025
Root & Branch Publishing

PB ISBN 978-1-0681782-1-4
eISBN 978-1-0681782-2-1

for

Ben

Josie, Fred, Louisa, Felix

and

Nic

X

Twits, Twitterers & Tweeters

as written in Bird Boy's notebook

Alcedo the Kingfisher
So fast he's a blur. Always watching. Always waiting. Probably knows more than any of us.

Chief Inspector Pica the Magpie
Loud. Dangerous. Thinks the garden belongs to him. It doesn't.

Cory the Greenfinch
Shy, but when she sings, even the trees lean in.

Grace and Alba the Ring-Necked Doves
Peaceful pair. Always together. I feed them now.

Sage the Parrot
Talks a lot. Most of it worth hearing.

Fruggie the Crow
A brave bird. I hope the others remember him the way I do.

Crook the Crow
Fierce. Secretive. Gone now.

Hula the Bullfinch
Loyal. Fierce. A natural leader with a soft spot for justice.

Major the Great Tit
Always shouting. Always brave. A tiny general with a big heart.

Merula the Blackbird
Swift and clever. If news spreads, it's probably from her.

Mr Blackbird
Delivers the leaf letters.
Parus the Blue Tit
So small. So fast. Still learning where the windows are!
Passer the House Sparrow
Tends to everyone. A feathery nurse with boundless energy.
Petra & Perseus the Peacocks
Vain. Loud. Flashy.
Phil the Song Thrush
Sings like he's smiling. Knows everyone's business but doesn't gossip.
Rube the Robin
Leader of the garden. Brave, even when afraid. I learned a lot just watching him.
Sergeant Pie the Magpie
Follows Pica. Carries out orders with relish.
Constable Peck
Brutal muscle, does the dirty work.
Starry the Starling
Hilarious. Loud. Can sound like anything — including cats, dogs, and the garden gate.

PROLOGUE

Bird Boy's Notes

Every morning when I climb up to my fort, the first thing I hear is the dawn chorus. It's one of the most beautiful sounds in the world — like nature's orchestra tuning up for sunrise. The birds sing together to mark their territory and call to their friends. Their songs grow louder and more exciting as the sun climbs higher, and when they all sing together, something magical happens.

They're stronger as a group than any of them could be alone.

I've been watching birds for ages now, drawing them and writing notes about their characters and habits in my special notebook. From my secret fort, I can see everything that happens in the garden, without anybody spotting me.

Magpies are one of the biggest threats to the smaller songbirds. Even though they eat lots of different things like insects and berries, they sometimes steal eggs and chicks from other birds' nests. I watched it happen from my fort last spring[RM1] . It was horrible. Magpies are tough and clever, but they don't seem to understand that the garden works best when everyone gets along.

The birds in our garden are amazing — full of adventures, friendships, and challenges that might surprise you! Sometimes, I write their adventures down. Not just the facts, but the way they might tell the story if they could.

chapter one

Rube the Robin

Rube nests low, in hidden places. He makes a new one every year. He likes shelves and flowerpots. I think he likes being near people.
— From Bird Boy's Notebook —

"Special delivery!" calls Mr Blackbird, crash-landing on my boat. No fancy loop-the-loop today, just a messy tumble of black feathers and scrambling claws.

"Important leaf-letter from Sage," he pants.

"What does she want this time?" I settle in for the usual news. "More May Day plans?"

Mr Blackbird shakes his head grimly. "Magpie

meeting. Dawn. All choir members must attend."

My tail feathers droop. Sage is next door's parrot. Her letters are usually fun — gossip about the humans, reminders about singing practice, and lists for our May Day party. But a Magpie Meeting?

"What do you think it means?" he asks, quietly.

Trouble. Big trouble.

"No idea," I say, ruffling my feathers. "But can you tell the others? I'd better get ready."

Before I fly off, let me introduce myself. I'm Rube — Rubecula Erithacus if you want to be fancy about it. I'm a robin with one of the brightest red breasts in all of Berkshire and lead singer of our local Songbird Choir. This is my patch: Riverside Garden at the end of Fishery Lane, where the garden slopes down to the river and the old boathouse. See that white rowing boat on the lawn? That's my headquarters, and it's the best command post a bird could hope for. I nest under the seat and keep watch over everything from this bow. At the moment, the apple trees are just finishing their blossom, and everywhere you look, the garden birds are busy with nests and eggs. It should be our happiest time of year.

But right now, Sage's leaf letter is suggesting we're in for a terrible day.

I make my usual pre-flight danger checks — look for hawks, scan for cats, locate the humans — then launch myself over the hedge to Sage's garden. The rest of the songbirds follow behind.

I take my position at the front of Sage's railing. The wise old parrot — my best friend, despite being ten times my size and not even a songbird — hops along her terrace towards me. Her humans let her roam freely out here, knowing that if any real danger appears, her screech will bring them running. The other singers line up and Sage gives a deep, dignified nod. I open with a clear trill, and the dawn chorus begins.

Parus, our youngest blue tit, careers in late. She tries to join the harmony but starts a beat early and sings a note too high, startling the sparrow next to her.

"Sorry! Got excited!" Parus chirps, puffing up her chest.

Hula, the bullfinch from two gardens up, rolls his eyes. I hide a smile. Parus means well.

Phil, the song thrush from Middle Garden, sings clear and loud as always, and the woodlark from The Mansion can't remain standing, drifting high above us with his sad but beautiful song. Sunlight peeps across the garden while Hula whistles and flutes, and the nuthatch from the other end of the lane pops up to a high perch for her loud, rhythmic delivery.

And that's when I notice them.

Black and white shapes, gathering on the rooftops.

More than usual.

Far more.

"Rube," whispers Phil, his voice faltering mid-note. "Look up there."

"Keep singing," I murmur back, though my voice wavers. "Don't let them know we've seen."

A rock dove, a pair of jackdaws, a starling, a green woodpecker, and lots of sparrows join in. There's even a heron, *kaharking* tunelessly along with the chorus. But the sky is darkening, and more birds are noticing now. Our melody becomes patchy as voices drop out.

"Eyes on me, everyone," calls Sage from her perch. "Music is hope. While we sing, we are free."

The magpies are circling, landing, waiting. Their silence scary against our joyful song.

The Titchies — blue tits, coal tits, long-tailed tits and their cousins — cluster together.

"So many magpies," breathes Parus.

"What do they want?" asks his friend.

The Finsters, our local finch gang, huddle together. A flashy, feisty flock of birds who are unusually subdued this morning. And Cory the greenfinch looks terrified.

I count the magpies gathering around us.

Thirteen.

Too many.

Something's definitely wrong.

chapter two

The Magpie Mafia

Magpies build big round nests high up. They use thorns so no one can get in.
They add to the same nest every year, until it's a fortress.
— From Bird Boy's Notebook —

Chief Inspector Pica, head of the Magpie Mafia, struts along the railing, glossy tail held high, black eyes glittering with something that makes my chest tighten.

He addresses us in his hoarse, ugly voice.

"First, a quick update on our excellent work, then we'll discuss some… changes to our arrangement."

Changes?

My throat goes dry. Magpies don't call meetings to discuss improvements.

"There are three new dogs in the road," Pica barks. "All huge, vicious — looking beasts. One is in Riverside Garden," — all eyes turn to me, and I give a long-suffering nod, though I can barely concentrate on his words — "and two next to Flamingo Tree Garden. These dogs look fierce, but they're lazy. So far, they just lie down and sleep when my patrol taunts them."

I try to focus, but that word *changes* is echoing in my head. A few sparrows twitter and tweet and are quickly silenced by a fierce *cha-ka* from Pica.

"Greater threats remain foxes, cats, small fluffy dogs. There are now only three foxes in the road. One fox was caught by my patrol, who lured it in front of a passing car by pretending to have a broken wing."

My stomach churns. I can barely listen to his bragging — all I can think about is what's coming next.

"The magpie officer responsible was Sergeant Pie," continues Pica. "Quite a feather in her cap."

Dutiful chirps and applause follow, and with a chilling chuckle, Pica turns to two magpies I don’t recognise.

"We had quite a feast that night, didn't we boys?”

I shudder. I don't mind the odd worm, but dead animals like that are another matter altogether. "Other than that," Chief Inspector Pica snarls, "we continue to protect all songbirds with our usual 'cat-call'."

I can hardly hear him for the hammering of my heart.

"Protection terms remain the same," Pica growls. "Our patrol will be out collecting the usual gifts from every garden — shiny things, scraps of food, whatever you've got. That's the deal. We keep the cats off your backs; you keep us happy."

I shift uncomfortably on the railing, my claws

gripping tight. This is how it's always been. The magpies provide protection from cats and other predators in exchange for 'gifts'. It's not ideal, but it works. Or at least, it has worked. But what did he mean by changes?

Pica pauses, his black eyes glitter, and every feather on my body stands on end.

"However," he continues, his voice taking on a harder edge, "things are changing on Fishery Lane."

Here it comes.

My breath catches in my throat.

"Three new magpie families have moved down from the northern counties — driven out by development, they tell me. My gang has nearly doubled in size."

He hops along the railing, and I notice more black and white shapes gathering on the rooftops than I've ever seen before.

"Feeding this many officers requires... adjustments

to our arrangement."

A terrible silence falls over the garden. Even the sparrows go quiet.

"From the end of next month," Pica announces, "protection payments will include the usual tributes, plus one egg per nest, per season. For everybody."

"An egg per nest?" whispers Parus.

I glance at Sage. Her yellow eyes meet mine with a slight shake of her head. *Stay quiet*, they seem to say.

"That's not fair!" chirps a sparrow.

"QUIET!" snaps Pica, his mean eyes look at all of us. "Songbird Choir members included."

I gasp, and open my beak to speak, but he hasn't finished.

He leans towards me, his breath sour, his voice low and cruel.

"And don't expect help from your humans," he hisses. "Your old one — Gunman we call him — shot two of my officers last year. He's bigger than any fox or cat — and ten times as deadly."

Birds gasp and ruffle their feathers. A few of the smaller sparrows actually fall off the railing in shock.

My legs go weak.

An egg per nest? That's not protection — that's theft.

That's taking our children.

An un-bird-like silence falls as Pica bounds off to join the other magpies.

"Goodbye, my friends," he rasps. "See you at the end of May."

And he glides away.

None of us dares speak. Everyone knows what happens if you don't pay the magpies. Last spring, they raided poor Merula's nest, after she refused.

I watch Pica and his gang of mean, humourless birds fly off towards the woods. Swooping, clicking, and whining. It's no surprise I've never heard a magpie sing. You have to feel joy to sing, and they are cold, joyless creatures.

Sage catches my eye one last time, her look saying what we both know — we'll figure this out together, like always.

We all scatter when the house door bursts open and Sage's dogs rush yapping into the garden. I am back on my boat in less than twenty wing beats, standing in my thinking place, pondering the dawn's events.

Four weeks. That's all the time we have to save our eggs. But I won't let Pica win. Not if I can help it.

chapter three

The Starlings

Starlings cram into roof spaces and boxes and chatter the whole time.
Sometimes they nest so close they argue in their sleep.
— From Bird Boy's Notebook —

The morning after Pica's terrible announcement, I wake before sunrise with Pica's words echoing in my head.

One egg per nest, per season.

Sleep was impossible with his threat clawing my thoughts, so I spend the early hours perched in the eucalyptus tree, watching and thinking.

As the first pale light creeps across the garden, I don't feel like singing. I can't summon even a single note. Instead, I sit in stunned silence, watching in awe as my friends somehow find the strength to continue their morning rituals. Phil's rich call echoes from the weather vane. The Titchies chatter softly as they search for seeds. Even little Parus manages a tentative *sisisi* from her nest box.

How can they carry on as if nothing has changed? Don't they realise that soon, everything we know might be destroyed? Or perhaps they understand something I don't — that clinging to normal routines is the only way to keep despair from swallowing us whole.

That's when I notice the starlings. They line up on *Gunman's* balcony railings like performers taking the stage, and I'm struck by something almost defiant in their mischief. Something that makes my chest tighten — not with fear this time, but with hope.

Silent as mice, still as ice, the starlings wait, their dark feathers gleaming with mischief.

It's barely dawn, the house is wrapped in sleep, but

the starlings have work to do.

"Ready, everyone?" Starry whispers.

A shiver of dissent, and they begin.

Starry starts the show, whistling a perfect imitation of *Gunman's* phone ringtone. Every beep and trill perfect.

"Brilliant!" chirps one of the younger starlings. "Now do the grumpy voice!"

The others join in with a chorus of "What now? WHAT NOW?" in exact imitation of *Gunman's* morning grouchiness.

"My turn!" calls another, and launches into a perfect copy of the coffee machine gurgling and hissing.

But Starry raises a wing for silence. "Save your energy for the masterpiece. One, two three…"

And every starling throws its head back and begins:

"DA — DA — DA — DA, DA — DA — DA — DA, DA — DA — DA — DA, DA — DA — DA —

DA!"

It's *Gunman's* alarm clock. Perfect pitch, perfect timing. And two hours early.

"Louder!" Starry commands.

They repeat it, their voices carrying through the still morning air. "DA — DA — DA — DA, DA — DA — DA — DA!"

A light flicks on inside the house.

"Yes!"

The starlings exchange delighted glances and launch into another round. When the window finally flies open, and *Gunman* appears — hair wild, face furious — the starlings scatter in all directions, squealing with joy.

"Mission accomplished!" Starry calls, his laughter echoing across the garden.

"Well done," I murmur, in awe of how clever the starlings are to do this. It isn't just random mischief, but carefully planned justice. Because later this morning,

Gunman will open that same window and fire at Grace and Alba — two gentle collared doves who've never hurt anyone.

Pica named him *Gunman* after the first bang echoed through the garden last spring. We've never seen a weapon, just heard the noise, but when Grace and Alba flee in panic, it's hard not to believe Pica's name is right. And so, until Bird Boy teaches his father the difference between friend and foe, we songbirds will continue our campaign of revenge.

Watching the starlings' prank, I find myself almost smiling for the first time since Pica's announcement. Their joy is infectious, their teamwork flawless. For a moment, I forget about the countdown ticking in my head. But as the laughter fades, Pica's threat creeps back like a shadow. Thirty days. I need something to lift my spirits, so I open my beak and let out a soft trill — nothing fancy, just a simple melody my father taught me about courage in dark times. The notes seem to chase away some of the fear until a magpie lands on the roof and makes my feathers tremble.

"Having fun?" asks Seargent Pie, Pica's right hand bird.

"What do you want?"

"Just checking our *'friends'* are behaving," she sneers. "Four weeks left, Robin."

She flies away, laughing, and I ruffle my feathers to shake off her threat. I need to focus on what matters — studying my friends' special talents. If we're going to survive what's coming, I need to think of uses for them.

In that spirit, I spot the sparrows gathering near the washing line later that morning.

"Is it our turn yet?" asks one of the younger birds, bouncing excitedly on a fence post.

"Patience," says his mother, Passer. "Wait until the washing's properly hung up."

"But I've been practicing my tightrope walking all week!"

"And your aim?" Passer asks with a knowing look.

"Bull's-eye every time!" the tiny bird puffs out his tiny chest proudly.

I chuckle despite my worries. Being so small and light, the sparrows can perch on the line without it sagging, and they have claimed it as their battlefield. The younger ones particularly enjoy walking along like tiny acrobats, and… well. Let's just say *Gunman's* laundry doesn't always stay pristine!

"Remember," Passer tells her youngsters, "only his clothes."

"I know, I know!" he chirps impatiently.

Their aim is remarkable — and hilarious.

But the sparrows aren't *Gunman's* only enemies. From high up in the oak tree, Cory the greenfinch calls down to me.

"Rube! The car's out! Roof down!"

"Excellent," I call back. "Sound the alert!"

Within moments, birds appear from everywhere. Our alert system works perfectly! Every member of our feathered family knows what to do — swoop and dump on the *Gunman's* precious car!

"Formation flying!" shouts Merula as she leads a group of blackbirds overhead.

"Target acquired!" calls Cory.

Though Grace and Alba tell us we shouldn't pester the man so much, we will continue to taunt him as long as he taunts them.

And our cheekiest revenge is yet to come.

"Wasp conference!" I announce later. Merula — our clever brown blackbird who always has the best ideas for mischief — flies over to join me.

"How's our no-interference policy working?" I ask.

Merula grins. "Beautifully. We now have the fattest,

happiest, most confident wasps in the neighbourhood. They think they own the garden!"

"And *Gunman*?"

"Oh, you should see him when the family eats outside!" Merula giggles. "The wasps go crazy around the food. *Gunman* jumps up and waves his arms like he's conducting our choir!"

I've seen it myself — the man leaping about, terrified of being stung, while his wife and children ignore the wasps and keep eating calmly.

"Poor Bird Boy tries so hard not to laugh," Merula adds with delight.

"And the sparrows take advantage?" I ask.

"Every time!" Merula laughs. "While he's dancing around, they sneak in and steal the food right off his plate. The chair droppings?"

"Passer's got the young ones practicing their aim daily. They never miss!"

Merula nods, but we both know *Gunman* is just a confused human. The magpies are organised, ruthless, and they know exactly what they're doing. Still, watching my friends work together gives me hope. Perhaps when the time comes, we'll find a way to turn our talents to a more serious purpose.

As I watch my friends in their daily routines — the sparrows' precision, the starlings' mischief, the wasps' boldness — I feel a bittersweet ache in my chest. This is what we're fighting for. Not just our eggs and nests, but these moments of joy, these small rebellions, this beautiful, chaotic community that somehow works despite everything.

I find myself humming softly — nothing fancy, just a simple tune about home. But even as I sing, Pica's threat echoes in my mind. How can we protect all this when we're so small, and they're so ruthless?

chapter four

Cory The Greenfinch

Cory nests in hedges. She makes a fresh one each spring.
She thinks if she stays still, she disappears.
— From Bird Boy's Notebook —

After thinking about the songbirds' strengths and skills, I decide to take stock of what we need to protect from the magpies. How many nests, how many eggs, how much time we have. So, I spend the rest of the afternoon calling birds over to my boat, one by one.

It feels good to have something practical to focus on.

Phil arrives first — big, spotted, and dependable.

He lands heavily on the bench.

"Second clutch," he says simply when I explain what I need. "Four eggs, due to hatch any day now. Perfect timing for May Day, I thought." His voice turns grim. "Though now I'm wondering if that was a mistake."

My stomach drops as I calculate. "Four weeks should be enough. Your chicks will be safely fledged by then."

Phil nods grimly before flying away. I watch him go, this steady, reliable friend and feel the weight of responsibility settling on my chest like frost. Four weeks. It sounds like forever, but I know how quickly time can slip away.

Hula arrives next, navigating carefully to my boat by sound, anger radiating from his bright red breast. The bullfinch lands with unnecessary force, making my boat shudder.

"Outrageous!" he bursts out. "One egg per nest! Highway robbery!"

"What's your situation?" I ask gently.

Hula's fierce expression softens for just a moment. "No nest this season. No partner would take on a blind mate — too risky when raising young." His voice hardens again. "But that doesn't mean I don't have skin in the game. Every chick in this garden matters to me. Phil's four, Cory's future clutch, little Parus when she finally gets going — they're all family."

I nod, understanding. Hula has always been the one listening for distress calls, using his keen hearing to spot dangers others miss, becoming the garden's early warning system. Without chicks of his own, he's become protector to them all.

"At least the others have four weeks to get their broods safely away," he continues, his eyes flashing. "But what if something goes wrong? What if the chicks are late to fledge, or the magpies come early? We can't just hope for the best. Someone needs to stand up to these bullies."

His anger frightens me — not because I think he'd hurt anyone, but because I recognize it. It's the same rage I feel when I think about Pica's cold eyes, his casual cruelty. At least Hula's anger burns bright and honest.

Major, the Great Tit from Maple Tree Garden arrives next, landing with a little salute.

"Excellent! A war council!" he says, striking a military pose. "We should discuss tactical approaches."

"Not now, Major. I'm trying to work out when all the chicks are due. What about your nest?"

"Two eggs. Should be hatching next week. A month should be plenty of time for them to fledge. But we still need tactics!" He puffs out his chest again. "We can't just sit around hoping for the best!"

His courage is infectious, even if his approach is

questionable.

"Any practical ideas?"

"Know your enemy. I'm going to out about these new magpies — where they roost, patrol patterns, weaknesses."

"Thank you, Major."

"Consider it done!" He salutes crisply.

Cory arrives quietly, her olive-green plumage catching the light as she flits nervously from branch to branch before finally settling on the edge of my boat. The little greenfinch hunches down, trying to make herself invisible, worry ruffling her feathers.

"I keep thinking about my sister," she mumbles.

"Your sister?"

"My sister lived in Maple Grove," Cory says quietly. "When the magpies came demanding eggs, she gave them her first clutch. But they kept wanting more."

"What happened?" I ask gently.

"She stopped laying altogether. Said she couldn't bear raising babies just to give them away." Cory's voice gets smaller. "She left that garden and never tried to nest again."

The weight of her words settles like a shadow. I want to sing something comforting, but what song exists for this? What melody can carry the promise that everything will be alright when I'm not sure it will be?"

"I was planning to start my clutch this week," Cory continues. "The timing seemed perfect — four weeks should be enough for them to hatch and fledge before… before the magpies come."

"That's the hope," I mutter.

"But what if something goes wrong? What if they're late hatching, or slow to fledge?" Her voice is barely a whisper. "Maybe it's safer not to try at all."

I can only offer the truth. "I'm scared too. But we'll face whatever comes together."

A slight smile touches her beak. "Together. That helps."

The pattern continues through the afternoon. Some birds are between broods; others have chicks nearly ready to fledge. I scribble my notes, trying to keep track of everyone's timings.

Parus bounces over last, practically vibrating with energy. "Oh, we're nowhere near ready! Just started building our nest yesterday. Won't even lay for another week!"

I drop my twig. A week to lay, then nearly two weeks to hatch, then three more weeks in the nest…

"That's over a month away, Parus."

"I know! Exciting, isn't it?"

My heart sinks. One bird, completely out of sync, could ruin everything. "Parus, that's well past the magpies' deadline. You'll have helpless chicks when they come collecting."

Her enthusiasm falters. "Oh. I hadn't thought… Maybe we should wait until next season?"

"No, wait - why don't you bring it forward? It's perfect timing! There are fat caterpillars everywhere. If you lay eggs in the next few days, your chicks will have flown the nest before the magpies come."

She practically bounces on her feet. "Brilliant. We'll finish the nest tonight!"

I try to look excited, but my heart isn't in it.. But at least I've given her the best chance.

As dusk approaches, Merula arrives, landing with efficient grace. "Lost my first clutch to the magpies three weeks ago," she says simply. "Five eggs. Haven't rebuilt yet - seemed pointless with May Day looming."

Her voice carries a weight I haven't heard before. Of all the birds in our choir, Merula has lost the most to magpies over the years.

"I've been talking to the sparrows from the terraced

houses," she continues. "Word's spreading about what's happening here. There might be other birds willing to help us, but it won't be easy."

I let out a trill of shrill laughter. "Too right it won't. It's hard enough to get the choir organised for practice, let alone arrange a battle we can never win." I shake my head firmly. "No, Merula. The answer isn't fighting — it's making sure there's nothing for them to steal. Empty nests by May Day. That's our only real option."

Merula tilts her head, studying me. "Maybe you're right. But what about birds like Parus? The late nesters?"

I don't have an answer for that, and we both know it.

As she flies into the gathering dusk, I feel pinned down by the weight of responsibility. Four weeks to save the next generation of songbirds.

It feels like forever and no time at all.

chapter five

The Titchies and The Finsters

Tits and finches like fluffy nests stuffed into holes and bushes.
You can always tell who built it by the mess.
— From Bird Boy's Notebook —

The next morning dawns clear and bright, a stark contrast to my troubled dreams. After yesterday's grim accounting, I'm grateful for the peaceful routine of my morning patrol.

But my peace explodes the second I get back to my boat. The Titchies hurtle towards me, screeching hysterically. I hop onto the deck, then fly to join them at the bird table.

"Rube! Rube!" chirps Parus. "We've seen aliens!"

I cover my face with my wings in mock horror. "Aliens?"

"Ask Phil. I need to go. Nests to build, eggs to lay!"

She flits away, twittering "Nesty, nesty nesty," then diverting to peck a juicy clump of moss from the willow tree.

Phil the song thrush appears by my side, his speckled breast catching the morning light. "They're not aliens," he says in his beautiful, clear voice. "But they're certainly different!"

"Good different?" I ask, peeping out reluctantly.

The Titchies giggle. It's nice to see them smile despite their worries.

"Yes. No. Well, strange different," chirps from somewhere in the bushes. "We were pecking at next door's seed feeder when we heard loud screeching from up the river."

"Don't tell me — more magpies?" I ask, my feathers bristling.

"No, no! Something else entirely! They're…"

The rest of her words are drowned out by The Finsters swooping in, chattering with excitement. They land with a flashy flourish, eager to beat The Titchies with the news.

"We saw them too," Cory says quietly, then clears her throat and speaks a bit louder. "They're… they're definitely feathery. I think they might be birds."

"Weirdest birds I've ever heard!" adds Hula boldly.

I hop onto a branch to listen properly. "What sort of weird?"

Parus bursts from the greenery, a trail of spider web dangling from her beak. "Enormous weird! One has a crown of blue and green feathers sticking straight up like he's wearing a fancy hat. The other has a tail that looks like someone stuck a huge rainbow fan to his bottom!"

Then she disappears.

The Finsters and Titchies burst into a twittering flap of excitement.

"Don't be ridiculous," I say, glancing at Phil and rolling my eyes.

"But we all saw them!" they chorus together, which is remarkable since they can't usually agree on anything.

Phil flies up to join me. "I flew over for a look myself," he admits. "They're in Maple Tree Garden. Very odd. Huge, colourful, and making quite a racket. But they seem peaceful. Not like the magpies."

Now I'm curious. And after Pica's threats, any distraction from our troubles is welcome.

"Well then," I say, stretching my wings, "I suppose as lead singer of the Songbird Choir, I should go and introduce myself properly."

"They don't sound much like singers," Phil observes. "More like they're having an argument with a rusty gate."

"We never judge," I reply firmly. "Singers of all abilities are welcome in our choir."

"Ooh, can we come with you?" calls Parus, from the bushes.

"You have more important work to do here," I say tactfully.

The Titchies and Finsters immediately start arguing about who gets to come and who has to stay on guard duty. I take advantage of their squabbling and flit across the hedge to see Sage and tell her about the new arrivals.

"Maple Tree Garden's a long way for a robin," she says. "And with the magpie threat hanging over us, it might be better if you stay close to home. Focus on preparing your defences." She pauses, her gaze growing distant. "My humans rescued me when I was little more than a chick," she continues, her voice taking on a softer quality. “My previous owners clipped my flight feathers, and they never grew back properly. I’ve learned to be careful about dangers.”

My heart sinks. I see her point, but I can't shake the feeling that these strange visitors might be helpful somehow.

"You're right," I sigh. "I suppose I should stay and work on our plans."

"I'll send out a leaf letter," Sage offers. “Someone else can investigate and report back."

chapter six

Hula the Bullfinch

Bullfinch nests are tidy and flat, low in a thicket.
They line them with hair.
Hula doesn't sing much, but he always listens.
— From Bird Boy's Notebook —

I spend the rest of the day pecking a countdown tally into the tree bark. One peck, one day. Twenty-six days until the magpies come. It doesn't look like much. Just a row of tiny notches, carved with mild panic and impeccable beak-work.

There's no official protocol for marking the approach of doom, so I make it up as I go. Peck a notch, take a bug break. Repeat.

The air is warming, and it smells like grass and fresh stone. Little bugs rise from the soil, and I hop about, snapping them up between tally breaks. Somewhere nearby, Sage is probably deciding who'll volunteer to greet the new arrivals. I wonder who'll be brave enough — or foolish enough — to step forward.

Then something catches my ear.

A voice. Familiar.

A soft, repeated *butt, butt* sound drifting from the direction of the hedge.

I pause, a fat worm dangling from my beak.

That's Hula's call, but what's he doing in my territory? And why does he sound so… panicked?

I drop the worm and fly towards the sound. Sure enough, there's Hula, perched on my fence post, his bright orange breast looking duller than usual, his deep, podgy bill poking out from his big round head. He's facing slightly away from me, head tilted as if listening for my approach.

"Oh, Rube," he says before I can even greet him properly.

"Hula? What are you doing here? You look terrible. What's wrong?"

His tail droops. "I volunteered to go and greet the aliens! I only did it because Major signed up, then The Titchies called me a coward. You know Rube, anything a Titchie can do, a finch can do better."

"They're not aliens," I say, in what I hope is a reassuring tone. "Phil's seen them. He says they're birds. Just not a species we recognise."

Hula ruffles his feathers. He might be a slow, sluggish bird, but he's kind and well-meaning and strong as an ox. "All you've got to do is fly up there and welcome them. If we can befriend them, maybe they can help with the magpie. And you'll be the hero of the choir for going to greet them."

"But what if they're not friendly?" Hula's long tail flicks up and down as he warbles anxiously. "What if they have special powers and attack me? What if I can't find them in time? What if I get lost out there in territory I don't know?"

Despite his size — Hula's almost half as big as me again — and his fighter's physique, he's a dreadful worrier. He looks tough and bright, but really, he's quite timid. He's clearly bitten off more than he can peck by volunteering for this mission. I know flying beyond his familiar routes is harder for him than it would be for most birds. Hula is strong and brave, but he can't see very well. The magpies took that from him two years ago — along with his mate and chicks. That's why he knows his territory by heart, and why flying somewhere new scares him. It's also why he hates the magpies more than any of us. The worst part is, he can't back out now.

The songbird community doesn't tolerate broken promises — your word is sacred, and once given, it must be kept. If Hula fails to show up, he'll be branded a coward and a promise-breaker. The shame alone could kill him.

Dusk will descend soon, and my reassurances to Hula are falling on deaf ears. The more I try to calm him, the more agitated he becomes. I watch his tail twitching frantically and feel something shift inside me. There's only one way to convince him to go through with this.

"Right then," I hear myself saying. "I'm coming with you."

Hula's head snaps towards my voice. "What?"

I ruffle my feathers nervously. Leaving my territory twice in one day goes against every robin's instinct I have. Plus, it's a very long flight for a little bird like me. But Hula needs me, and despite his flaws, he's my friend.

The decision surprises me, but feels right. As we prepare to leave, I find myself humming quietly — a traveling song my mother used to sing. It's meant for migration, for journeys into the unknown. Hula's battered head turns towards the sound, and for the first time today, his shoulders relax slightly.

"You heard me. We'll meet Major together — I'll help you navigate."

For the first time since he arrived, Hula's expression brightens slightly. "You'd really do that? But Rube, your territory…"

"Will still be here when I get back." I hope.

And this is how I find myself flying upstream with Hula into the gathering dusk. I stay close to his left wing, calling out landmarks as we go.

"Oak tree coming up on your right. Stream bends left here. Watch for the telephone wires." The wind picks up as we fly, ruffling our feathers and carrying the scent of approaching rain. By the time we reach our meeting place in the maple tree, dark clouds are gathering overhead.

I sigh, watching Hula's nervous fidgeting beside me as he orients himself by the familiar creak of the maple's branches.

This is going to be a long night.

chapter seven

Peacocks!

Peacocks don't nest in trees.
They just sit around like they own the place.
I think they forget how big they are.
— From Bird Boy's Notebook —

Major's waiting for us, perched on the highest branch like he owns the tree.

"You're late," he says.

He's bigger than me but smaller than Hula. His black head has white patches on the cheeks, and his yellow and black belly makes him look like a soldier. A fine feathered specimen. And he knows it.

Dark clouds are gathering above us, and we must hurry if we are to complete our mission before nightfall.

We all swoop to the ash tree for a better view, scanning the garden below. The lawn is empty, the shadows quiet.

"Where are they?" whispers Hula tilting his head and listening intently.

“In that dog kennel,” says Major. “But I’ll soon get them out.”

He flies to the middle of the lawn and calls in his loudest *che-che-che-che* voice, sounding almost like a magpie. Amazingly, this simple strategy works!

Two enormous, shiny creatures saunter from the kennel under the kitchen window. My beak drops open. They're twice the size of any bird I've ever seen, walking across the lawn in silence, tipping their tiny heads from side to side.

"Incredible," Hula breathes beside me. "I can hear them walking — they're massive!"

They are odd creatures, with head crests (not lasers).

Definitely feathered but with no sign of the silly 'rainbow fan' described by The Titchies.

"Peacocks!" calls Major, flying to a higher, safe position to address the visitors. "Good evening! We are from the Songbird Choir," he announces, striking a pose. "We have come to welcome you to the neighbourhood."

I am so busy gawping at the magnificent birds, I don't notice Hula growing restless beside me. He's been quiet since we arrived in Mapple Tree Garden, probably feeling overshadowed by Major's pomposity. I should have realised he was struggling to see the peacocks clearly in the gathering dusk. Determined to prove himself, he flies behind them and lands on their kennel with a loud thump, draws breath and whistles the first three notes of our choir's warm-up trill — *chee-cheep-cheep* — but he never gets the fourth out before the peace of the evening explodes into squawks and screeches.

Silly Hula. He must have been so focused on showing off for Major, he forgot to make the usual pre-landing danger checks — harder for him to spot threats in the dim light. Before he knows what's happening, a sleek shadow shoots from the open window. A cat. Its emerald-green eyes narrowing into cold slits that gleam in the fading light, its paws out for balance — and its claws out for poor Hula.

Then everything scatters into chaos. The first peacock lets out a blood-curdling scream that makes my feathers stand on end. His tail fans out like a shield covered in staring eyes, and he lunges at the cat with surprising speed. The second male raises his own magnificent tail and attacks with fierce, claw-like spurs.

Hula breaks free and flies to safety. "Where? Which way?" he calls, struggling to orient himself in the commotion. But Major, trying to help, has flown too close to a hedge. The cat spots him and crouches low, blocking his escape route. Major is trapped.

In a desperate attempt to save everyone, I throw myself to the ground. I land hard on my side and lie, weakly fluttering a wing, making my most pitiful dying call.

The cat pauses and pricks its evil ears. Then it turns, spoiled for choice by this sudden menu of songbirds all waiting to be its next meal. Then it crouches low, whiskers twitching with anticipation, and starts creeping towards me.

My heart hammers against my scarlet breast, but I wait, and wait, until finally, Major's voice cuts through the darkness.

"MISSION ABORT!"

And I am up and off, my heart still hammering as I fly high above the gardens.

“Thank you!” I call down to the peacocks as we escape.

“Cats are our enemies too!” one shouts back. “We don’t like bullies!”

“This way, Hula!" I call out, guiding him home through the darkening sky. The familiar trees of Riverside Garden have never looked so welcoming.

***

Back home, I settle down to roost, and replay the evening's pandemonium in my mind. The way that first peacock screamed and lunged at the cat. Those powerful, claw-like spurs on the second male… I've never seen anything like it. Even the cat — a predator that strikes fear into every songbird — was terrified.

My drowsy thoughts drift to our magpie problem. Pica and his gang think they're the toughest birds around, but if those peacocks can squawk a cat into retreat, what might a garden of songbirds do — if we ever dare to raise our voices together?

chapter eight

Bird Boy

I don't have a nest. Not a real one.
But I know where everyone else does.
That counts.
— From Bird Boy's Notebook —

Twenty-five days until the magpie raid. That's what the tally says.

I checked it this morning — ran my beak across the bark and counted twice, just to be sure. Still twenty-five.

Which means, technically, there's time.

Time to take a breath.

Time to pretend everything is normal.

And besides, May Day is only four days away. Sage says no one's allowed to worry until after the celebration. "Doom can wait," she said this morning, bossing a pair of sparrows about vine streamers while clutching a leaf list of competitions in her scaly feet.

There's going to be a prize for Best Nest Lining, one for Shiniest Plumage, and a special relay race where teams carry feathers across the lawn without dropping them.

The whole garden will be decorated in wild garlic blossoms, ivy ropes and catkins. And the river birds are rehearsing some sort of water ballet.

So I've made a deal with myself: I'll worry later. After the bug buffet and the berry garlands. After the songbirds sing their socks off. For now, I'm focusing on lighter things. Worms. Secrets. And this mysterious business in the flowerbed.

It's the weekend. I know this because our human children aren't at school. Weekends are a bit of a bother for us songbirds, as the five human children take over the garden as if they own the place. They shout, crash into things and forget where they left their sandwiches.

A nightmare, really. But also, a catering opportunity.

Another good thing about weekends is that our special child – Bird Boy – fills the seed feeders, stocks the bird table and generally checks that things are in order for us. Bird Boy is different from all other humans. He's nine years old with sandy hair that sticks up in all directions. While his siblings charge around making noise, Bird Boy moves quietly and carefully, always watching us with those keen green eyes of his — eyes that miss nothing, not even which tree we sleep in, who's stolen the last crust from the table, or which birds sing first in the dawn chorus. I've even seen him timing when the migrants arrive each season. And he writes it all down in a special notebook he carries everywhere. Sometimes, Bird Boy even tries to whistle to us. It's a flat, breathy squeak, but I puff my chest and pretend it's a masterpiece. It seems only polite.

On this particular day, there is much fuss and excitement. *Gunman* and his wife drag a series of enormous boxes into the garden. Then *Gunman* and the three boys set about opening them, while the mother and two girls get out the garden tools and begin clearing a space in the flower bed.

Of course, I am over there straight away. Sage tells me humans think robins are tame. We're not tame. We're just not afraid of humans — which is very different. Also, we know that wherever there's a human, there's food.

For example, now. The fresh dirt around *Gunman* smells rich and damp, like the ground after a good rain. He's tossing bits of grass and flower roots into the air, and little worms are wiggling up into the light. Phil comes to join me, though he keeps glancing back toward his territory, tail flicking restlessly. We hop around in the broken soil, flicking dirt and feasting like kings while pretending not to watch each other's technique. Phil pauses to crack a snail against a nearby stone, the sharp *tap-tap-tap* echoing across the garden. but even as he works, his head keeps jerking up, listening.

“My mate's doing her best," he says between strikes, "but she's not used to being alone on the nest for long stretches. I should get back soon."

The family's mysterious project doesn't hold Bird Boy's attention for long, and soon he wanders off to his secret fort. From there, he can see the entire garden. It's the perfect place to watch birds, but I've seen him with his ear to the ground too, listening to things most humans don't bother with. In the fort, he's hidden from his family, tucked away behind the yew hedge beneath sycamore boughs, but we birds know exactly where he is. We've all been inside when he's not there. He has a log seat, bird books, binoculars, a map of the nature reserve and a notebook.

Whenever Bird Boy's in his fort, I make sure different types of birds fly past to keep him entertained. Occasionally I even manage to organise a 'rare' sighting for him. Last year, a green woodpecker agreed to drum in the tree above him. Though the woodpecker was too shy to show herself, clever Bird Boy identified the sound immediately and scribbled excitedly in his book before rushing to show his father.

I think Bird Boy's preparing for May Day too. I spotted him earlier carrying a small blue tub. He left it on the stump near the feeder and when I checked, it was full of mealworms. He brings them out for special occasions. Like birthdays. Or Tuesdays. Or when he's had a good day.

Today passes gently, and I manage to do a good job of pretending I'm not worried. Bird Boy stays in his fort. The other humans dig, hammer and argue about instructions. The bird table provides toast crusts in the morning, and what looks like a piece of fish finger in the afternoon.

It is, in short, an excellent distraction.

As the day wears on, the humans' project begins to take shape. It is a tiered fountain and bird bath. A perfect place for us to gather, bathe and drink in the summertime. The songbirds will be thrilled. Sage will probably insist on a lifeguard rota. And with May Day just three days away, the timing couldn't be better. It will be the ideal occasion for a launch. Maybe even a ribbon. I'll suggest it to Sage.

While I'm monitoring progress on our exciting new bird bath, the human mother calls her children inside for dinner. *Gunman* is left alone, kneeling in the middle of the flowerbed, connecting the last pieces of the fountain. He spots me watching, and his eyes widen, just like Bird Boy's.

"Hello, you magnificent creature," he says, throwing me his apple core to peck.

I happen to love apples. And I am, quite obviously, magnificent.

Perhaps *Gunman* isn't so bad after all.

chapter nine

Magpie Warning

Magpies watch the nests.
They remember where the eggs are.
— From Bird Boy's Notebook —

The next day I wake with a flutter of excitement in my chest. Three days until May Day! The most magical morning of the year, when every bird in the garden joins together in the ancient dawn chorus that welcomes spring properly into the world.

I've been looking forward to this for weeks — the one day when our voices unite in something bigger than ourselves, bigger than our individual worries.

But this morning, something feels… still. The kind of still that usually means a hawk overhead. I shake it off. Probably nothing. Just nerves. May Day is nearly here.

Twenty-four days left on my magpie tally, but this morning my heart is light with anticipation. Soon we'll have our celebration.

I'm just stretching my wings, already hearing the opening notes of our May Day song in my head, when Starry and his flock swoop over my boat towards *Gunman's* balcony. Their familiar dawn performance drifts across the garden — phone ringtones, grumpy voices, and that perfect alarm clock imitation that never fails to enrage its target.

I've grown so accustomed to the starlings antics, I barely glance up anymore. Their defence of Grace and Alba has become as regular as sunrise itself. Impressive, of course, but just part of our garden's daily rhythm. In the background, the Gunman's angry shouts drift from his window and the starlings giggle and scatter, bringing a smile to my beak.

But my amusement dies when I spot a leaf letter waiting on my boat bench. The distinctive black scratches of Pica's talon work are unmistakable, and my heart pounds with dread. So while Phil tweets and twitters in the flowerbed nearby, I read Pica's message, and feel my world collapse.

"The black and whites are coming," I stutter, my voice barely audible.

Phil the song thrush flaps over to join me, then hops sideways along the branch. "I know. But we've got twenty-four days. You worked it all out. Most of the chicks will be fledged by then, and the late nesters will delay."

— *I'd trusted him. Foolish I know. But he gave us a*

timeline and I clung to it like it meant something—

My talons grip the letter so tightly it tears.

All my careful calculations. All that hope. Worthless.

"No" I say, my voice shaking. "This week. Listen. *'Our timelines have changed, and we will now be visiting to take what we're owed at the end of this week.'*"

"This week!" Phil shrieks, his voice loud enough to carry across ten gardens.

"That's in three days," I mutter, the full horror sinking in.

"But my babies will have just hatched..."

— *Why warn us? I don't know. Maybe he enjoys watching us squirm. Make us sweat. Pica likes his victims scared— it's part of the fun.*

Phil's voice turns bitter. "They planned this all along. They lied from the beginning to give us false hope. Now they'll find more eggs and chicks in our garden than at any other time of year."

Just as I think things can't get any worse, a voice cuts through the morning, making my blood run cold.

"Our timelines have changed."

It's Pica! Come to gloat I suppose.

I whip around, fired up to challenge the black and white bully, but all I can see is Starry, alone on the fence post. His head tilts as he speaks again, in the exact pitch of Chief Inspector Pica.

"The end of this week," he growls, then shakes his feathers and tries again. "We will now be visiting to take what we're owed." He has captured Pica's cold, commanding tone perfectly.

I shake away the shock, and turn back to Phil. "We need an all-choir alert," I say. "Can you announce the news to the other songbirds? An emergency, daylight meeting."

"Daylight. Oh Rube, are you sure? Can't we wait until dusk?"

"No! There's no time to lose!" The urgency crashes over me. "Just yesterday, Cory saw three magpies circling Copper Beech Garden. And the day before that, Merula found the Beech Tree robin's nest completely destroyed. They're already collecting, Phil. They're on their way."

The air feels heavy and still, as if the whole garden is waiting for something terrible to happen. Even the leaves on the trees stop rustling.

chapter ten

Starry the Starling

Starry nests in the roof with her family.
Too many feathers. Too many feet. Too much fun.
— From Bird Boy's Notebook —

"Daylight meeting on the roof of the boathouse immediately," declares Phil in a shrill, urgent cascade of notes guaranteed to reach even the deaf old ears of Grace and Alba. "One attendant per family, everybody else to act as lookouts."

"A daylight meeting! A daylight meeting" shriek the starlings in an exact mimic of Phil's announcement.

The response is immediate. A rush of wings fills the

air as birds pour from every corner of the garden — finches from the oak tree, sparrows from the hedge, thrushes from the flower beds. They land with soft thuds and scratching claws on the wooden roof. The old timber creaks under dozens of tiny feet. Wings fold with whispered rustles and the gentle sounds of settling — a shift here, a hop there, as they find their places — gradually fade into expectant stillness.

The gathered birds fall silent as I land — dozens of them, representing every family in our garden community. Their eyes are fixed on me, hoping for leadership, for answers I don't have.

"Friends," I begin, my voice barely steady. "I've called you together because we've received word from Chief Inspector Pica. The protection payment we thought we had nearly a month to prepare for…" I pause, seeing hope in their eyes that I'm about to crush. "They're coming in three days. This Friday. May Day."

The silence is deafening. Then Major speaks, his voice sharp with outrage. “But my babies will have just hatched..."

"I know," I whisper. "That's exactly what Pica planned. He lied to us about the timeline. He wants to find our gardens at peak nesting season, when there are more eggs and chicks than at any other time of year."

A wave of horrified whispers ripples through the crowd.

"So, what do we do?" asks Major.

I look out over all these brave faces, turned towards me in the morning light. My friends. My community. All waiting for me to have an answer.

I don’t.

***

The garden falls silent after my announcement. Even the trees and the water in the new fountain seem to hold their breath.

Bird Boy notices the quiet. He goes to his fort and watches us nervously, the scratch-scratch of his pencil on paper the only sound as he scribbles in his little notebook, writing faster than usual, as if he's trying to solve a puzzle only he can see.

The songbirds fly back to tell their families the terrible news — the magpies are coming for payment. The silence doesn't last. First come quiet peeps, then calls and cries that echo off the water. Finally, there's a frenzy of flapping as every bird in Riverside Garden starts preparing for the magpies' raid, filling the air with the whoosh of wings and the sharp scent of fear.

I catch Starry's eye and gesture towards him urgently. "Starry," I call quietly, barely above a whisper. "Need you here. Now."

He hops closer.

"Listen carefully," I say, my voice hushed but insistent. "If this comes to a fight, you might be our only weapon. I need you to practice some exact phrases — get them perfect, but do it downstream, away from the main garden. We can't risk any magpie scouts overhearing."

Something makes me look up then, and my blood runs cold. Across the river, on the far bank, a lone magpie is perched on a dead branch. Constable Peck. Her black eyes are fixed directly on us, watching. Waiting. A chill runs down my spine.

"Quick," I whisper even more quietly, moving to block the magpie's view of Starry. "The key Pica commands: 'Stand down immediately!' 'Return to base — urgent orders!' 'Mission aborted!' Practice until they sound exactly like Pica's voice."

Starry nods grimly, understanding immediately. "I'll get them right, Rube. I promise."

"Good. Now call the others — all of them. But be subtle about it."

Starry lets out a series of low, warbling calls that seem to ripple outward like stones thrown in still water. At first, nothing happens. Then the sky begins to darken. Clouds of starlings approach from every direction. The musty smell of feathers fills the air, along with the whistle of countless wings cutting through the sky.

They land everywhere — on the boathouse roof with thunderous scratching of claws on weathered wood, on the jetty posts, along the riverbank. The old wood creaks and groans under their weight. Starlings come from upstream, downstream, and even from across the river, though they give Constable Peck a wide berth. Wherever I look, the sky is shimmering with birds, their murmurs creating a low, vibrating hum.

Once they find places to perch, the starlings fall unusually quiet, waiting for Starry's instructions. I glance back at the far bank — Peck is still there, still watching.

"Tell them what's coming," I whisper to Starry. "But keep it quiet. We’re being watched.”

chapter eleven

Fruggie the Crow

Crows builds high up in old trees.
They reuse their nests, but always add something new. Like a crown. Or a key.
— From Bird Boy's Notebook —

I need advice — someone who's seen more seasons than the rest of us combined.

The sharp scent of hawthorn brushes my feathers as I fly through the hedge into next door's garden.

Sage is waiting on her railing. Her green plumage has dulled with age, but her eyes are as bright and knowing as ever. She turns her head towards me as I land.

"What are you going to do?" she asks simply.

"I don't know. We've only got three days. I'd suggest abandoning ship, but the nests..." The words tumble out in a rush.

"Slow down. Breathe," she says. "Think about what you songbirds can do that magpies can't."

My mind begins to race.

"What, you mean apart from sing?"

Sage dips her head. "Yes, apart from sing."

"Well, there's the starling's mimicry, the sparrows' acrobatics, Cory's surveillance..." I pause, hearing how desperate I sound. "But they're still just songbirds, aren't they? What can a few sparrows do against a group of huge magpies?"

"A single sparrow can't stop a hawk, but a hundred sparrows together can turn the sky dark."

"What do you mean?"

"Your birds, Rube. Your little community." She stretches one clipped wing as far as it will go. "You need to pull together. Ask your friends for help. Create an army."

"An army? In three days?"

"I've already contacted the river birds. And there's a brave crow from Flamingo Tree Garden who's agreed to search for goshawks — they're one of the few predators that actually frighten magpies. Apart from Gunman — and we know we can't count on him."

I shiver, a chill seeping through my feathers. "I'll believe that when I see it. Magpies aren't afraid of anything."

Sage's eyes gleam like chips of amber in the morning light. "Maybe that fearlessness will be their downfall. When you're not afraid of anything, you don't prepare for everything."

"I hate how arrogant Pica is," I burst out, my voice crackling with frustration. "He knows we can't fight back. I'm no bigger than his head!"

"Think about it, Rube. Now go. Speak to the crow."

Her words echo in my mind as I launch myself into the air. The flight feels longer than usual, each wingbeat carrying me further from the safety of our riverside home and deeper into uncertainty.

The air smells different in Flamingo Tree Garden — earthier, with hints of exotic blooms unfamiliar to me. I'm not usually a fan of crows — they make me feel small, but this one might just save our lives, so I have to be brave and represent our community with my thanks.

I hear the huge bird before I see him. His harsh, raspy caws echo through the garden's twisted branches, and I follow the sound past flowerbeds releasing the sweet, heavy perfumes of spring and find him by the compost heap.

"My name is Fruggilegus," he croaks as I announce my arrival with a tentative chirp. He's in terrible shape. One leg hanging at an odd angle, blood crusted around his talons. His eyes are swollen, the lids heavy with infection. His feathers have lost their shine.

I've never seen a crow in such terrible condition.

"Rubecula," I reply, then, worried I'm sounding pompous, I add, "But call me Rube. And I'll call you Fruggie because your name is a bit of a beakful."

Fruggie explains that his colony has rejected him. "Crows are flock birds," he says quietly, his words barely rise above the whisper of wind through leaves. "We do everything together — hunting, roosting, warning of danger. Being cast out has meant…" He trails off, looking at his injured wing.

I can smell loneliness on him like old rain.

"And you're planning to fly solo to Cliveden Woods? Three miles. In that state?" I chirp, hopping from foot to foot on the rough bark beneath me.

"Might as well do what I can. Sounds like you songbirds have a big problem. You won't be able to hold back the magpies alone, but if I can bring the goshawks, you're sorted." He pauses, gazing at the earth. "Plus, if my colony hear I've done something so brave, maybe they'll take me back."

"That would be good," I twitter, tilting my head and catching the faint scent of hope lifting from his damaged feathers.

"Exactly." His eyes brighten with fierce determination, cutting through the gathering shadows. "It's dangerous, but it's my only chance. And there's no time to lose," he croaks, spreading his good wing with a sound like leather stretching. The injured wing hangs limp, trailing a few loose feathers that drift to the ground. "I'll leave at dusk — fly through the night. If I can reach the woods by dawn, I might be lucky and hear their call."

"Do you even know where the goshawks live?" I chirp, my voice barely audible above the settling sounds of evening — the distant splash of a fish jumping, the rustle of small creatures in the undergrowth.

"No, but I'll caw an all-bird alert as I travel. Maybe somebirdy will point me in their direction. I just hope I can find them in time." His voice carries the desperation of a creature with nothing left to lose.

I droop my wings and hop around, feeling useless beside his broken magnificence.

"You're very brave," I say, hopelessly.

"Brave or foolish — probably both," he says with a sad chuckle that sounds like pebbles rolling in his throat.

"What you're doing for our community is incredible. Is there anything we can do for you in return?"

"Well, there is something. But you shouldn't do it alone…" His words hang in the air, heavy with his exhaustion and the risk he's about to ask of me.

I nod, more confidently than I feel, my red breast

trembling in the cooling air.

"If I don't return in two dawns, could you tell my colony where I went? And why?"

My beak opens happily, but my heart feels heavy as stone. "Of course."

"And promise me something else, Rube. If the goshawks do come — when they come — remember that good can come from the darkest moments."

"I don't understand."

"You will," he says softly, his voice carrying the gentle warmth of someone who has found peace with their choice. "Even if I don't make it back, at least I'll have tried to do something that matters."

"Good luck, Fruggie." I watch him struggle to spread his wings, one hanging uselessly while the other beats with fierce determination. Part of me wants to fly alongside him, but we both know this is something he must do alone.

chapter twelve

Parus the Blue Tit

Parus finds the tiniest hole and squeezes in.
Once I saw a blue tit nest in a boot.
— From Bird Boy's Notebook —

Our second-to-last day of peace arrives with cruel sunshine. Every bird — and Bird Boy too — busy battening down the hatches. I spot him dragging a huge net and some string into his fort, and later he's up a tree with those binoculars again, scanning along the river like a scout.

"There's still one over there," Phil calls down quietly from the weather vane, his speckled chest clearly visible against the sky. "That magpie on the dead tree — she's been watching us all morning."

I look across the river. There she is, Sergeant Pie, sitting perfectly still, staring right at us.

"Just ignore her," I whisper to the others.

Phil and Merula take turns keeping lookout from the weather vane. Both have the loudest warning calls in our community. "I don't think he's going anywhere," Phil adds sadly. "My mate's with the chicks, but I hate leaving them to keep watch up here."

No one talks about it, but everyone remembers what the magpies did to their families.

There's no time to stop and chat with birds from other flocks, but I can see the starlings have split into two groups. Starry looks over at me and tries to smile, but I can tell he's worried too. What can a bunch of starlings do against a whole gang of magpies?

Each is rehearsing a different call, their voices rising and falling like distant sirens. The Titchies are busy stuffing their secret stores with beech nuts from next door's copper tree. "At least we'll have food when we're hiding," one of them says, trying to sound cheerful.

The finch cocks are looping in perfect flying patterns, while the hens gather red rubber bands left carelessly on the road by the postman. They're practicing their flying, but everyone knows it won't be enough if the magpies come in force.

Grace and Alba are nowhere to be seen. I'll check on them later. Right now I need to focus on the garden — on what must be done — but my eyes keep drifting across the river, towards the woods.

Is Fruggie still flying?

Is he hurt?

Will I really have to go to his colony if he doesn't return?

I don't want to think about it. But I can't stop.

The morning drags on, each minute feeling like an hour.

Then just as the sun reaches its peak, it happens.

Parus, who has been going at it beak and feather since dawn, veers off course and slams straight into the glass door of the house with a terrible thud.

She drops to the deck like a stone and lies there — no bigger than a bumblebee — senseless and still. From behind the glass, the huge dog barks and scrabbles, wild-eyed and furious.

"Oh no," I whisper. "No, no, no."

We all freeze. *Gunman's* heavy boots clomp towards the door. He peers out, sees Parus lying helpless on the ground, and disappears back into the house.

"He's getting his gun," someone mutters.

The door clicks. It opens. *Gunman* steps out.

I can't watch.

I cover my eyes with one wing.

Please no. Not Parus.

But the silence stretches too long, and I force

myself to look.

And there it is.

Gunman, sitting on the garden step, cradling Parus in a cloth in the palm of his huge hand. And he is making the loveliest sound — a kind of cooing. Like a parent, with a sick chick.

"Come on, little lady," he murmurs. "You can do it."

Parus lies there for a moment, blinking, dazed.

Then — miracle of miracles — she stands. Wobbly at first. She cocks her head left, then right, left, then right again.

"There you go," *Gunman* breathes.

He lifts his hand to the sky. Parus spreads her wings and flutters away into the eucalyptus tree.

Sisisi, sisisi, sisisi she sings, before fluttering up to a branch near the swing.

chapter thirteen

Major the Great Tit

Major nests in the bird box near the shed.
He guards it like a soldier.
No one else goes near it.
— From Bird Boy's Notebook —

Even Parus's recovery can't lift the weight pressing down on my chest.

Two days.

We have two days left.

As I watch the little blue tit settle into his nest, still shaking the dizziness from his tiny head, I know we need every advantage we can get for what's coming.

I sit on the bow of my boat, brain going round and round. Sage told me to think bigger. Create an army.

Fruggie the crow is looking for goshawks, but what if he fails? What if we need even more?

Then I remember something. The day we went to welcome the peacocks. Their horrible screams. Piercing shrieks that echoed across the entire garden, so loud it seemed to pierce my skull and make my beak ache. Even the cat ran away when they started their awful chorus. If just the screams can scare a cat, imagine what they'd do to a magpie! Even Pica will be scared of them.

My heart starts beating fast. Think bigger, Sage said. Bigger than crows. Bigger than goshawks.

Peacocks!

But who should approach them? Everybody is too busy preparing for the magpie attack.

Then I hear a familiar *teacher-teacher* call from the flowerbed.

It's Major, looking for caterpillars. He would be the perfect bird.

I fly to join him and he stops, puffing his chest out importantly. Out of the corner of my eye, I catch a glimpse of black and white in the oak tree — another magpie spy, silent and watching. My heart hammers against my ribs. They've been everywhere since they ramped up the timeline.

“Rotten business with these magpies. Anything I can do, let me know," Major says.

"You read my mind," I whisper, hopping onto a pine cone to bring me up to his height and nodding towards the oak. "I have a job that requires courage and exceptional diplomatic skills."

Major's eyes brighten. "Go on."

"The peacocks," I say quietly, letting the words hang in the air.

He bristles. "Flashy show-offs, if you ask me. All feathers and no substance."

"Exactly why we need someone of your caliber to

approach them," I continue, tilting my head seriously. "Someone who won't be intimidated by their… theatrical displays. Someone with real authority."

“Well naturally,” Major preens. Continue.” His chest feathers puff out so far, he’s nearly twice his normal size.

"When the magpies arrive in two days, we'll need all the help we can get. The peacocks have impressive voices —their calls can be heard for miles. If they would agree to raise the alarm when they spot the magpies passing their garden, it could give us vital advance warning."

Major straightens to his full height. "And you think I'm the bird to convince them?"

"I don't think, Major. I know. You have a way with words, a commanding presence. If anyone can make them see reason, it's you."

Major's beak gleams. "Well, naturally. When do you

need me to go?"

"Now, if you're willing. Time is of the essence."

Major spreads his wings with a flourish. "Consider it done, Rube. I'll have those peacocks squawking our warning calls by sunset. Leave it to me — I'll sort this out properly. I'll alert the whole garden!"

And with that, he launches himself into the air with all the self-importance of a general heading to negotiate a treaty.

Less than an hour later, Major returns.

His chest isn't puffed out and his head's hanging low. He lands heavily on my boat without his usual flair.

"Well?" I ask, though my sinking heart suggests I already know the answer.

Major clears his throat uncomfortably. "Ah, yes. Well. The thing is…" He pauses, ruffles his feathers, and tries again. "The peacocks were…unreceptive."

"Unreceptive?"

"They laughed." Major's voice is barely above a whisper. "Actually laughed. Said they don't get involved in *'common garden squabbles'* and that making warning calls was *'beneath their station.'*"

My heart sinks further. "Anything else?"

Major winces. "They… they said if I was so worried about garden birds, perhaps I should consider finding myself a '*more suitable neighbourhood.'* And then they said something very strange."

"What?"

"They said, *'We don't do warnings, little bird. We do action.'*"

I have no idea what that means, but something in Major's tone makes my tail feathers prickle with unease.

Major shakes his head miserably. "I think they were threatening me. As if warning calls weren't good enough for the likes of them."

The silence that follows is deafening. Even the

sparrows stop their chattering.

"I see," I say finally, trying to keep the disappointment from my voice. “It seems we're on our own."

chapter fourteen

Merula the Blackbird

Merula builds her nest close to the ground, tucked in ivy or brambles.
She acts like she doesn't care, but she's always watching.
— From Bird Boy's Notebook —

Dawn rises with a feeling of dread today.

Tomorrow the magpies come.

With spirits so low, I decide a rousing chorus is needed. Though I usually prefer to deliver my song from a concealed position, today is not the day for shyness.

I fly to the gate at the centre of the river fence,

cock my tail, curtsy, and begin. Phil joins me first, his rich tenor blending with my melody. Then Merula adds her flute-like notes.

Soon The Titchies, The Finsters, and the house sparrows join our chorus. The starlings take their position on their now favourite boathouse roof, and even Grace and Alba rise to the chorus and fly onto the fence to join us. We sing until the very sky bursts with music, and the sun rises across the river, shining its sleepy rays onto Riverside Garden.

Fruggie has not returned. Two dawns, he said. I sit on my boat, wings drooped, looking anxiously into the sky. There is so much to do and so little time. A promise is a promise, I know, but today of all days would be the worst time for me to leave my territory, and in truth, I'm afraid.

The fears crowd my mind like storm clouds.

I'm afraid that the magpie mafia will massacre my

friends and their children.

I'm afraid of flying all the way to the nature reserve, having never been that far from my nest before.

And I'm afraid to approach the crow colony, knowing that if they choose, they could make mealworm of me in seconds. Again, I look to the skies towards the Cliveden Woods, but there is no Fruggie and no inspiration, just a dark, menacing cloud rolling slowly upstream towards my beloved Riverside Garden.

I go to see Sage, and she agrees that I must go to the nature reserve and give Fruggie's message to the crow colony as I have promised. It is a matter of honour, she explains, though I can tell it pains her to say so. It is, without doubt, a hazardous journey.

Two flaps and a glide and I'm back at my boat, calling Phil to tell him my plans. Mr Blackbird flies over on his postal path and drops me a leaf letter. I curtsy my acknowledgement and continue talking to Phil.

"Pica and his gang will most probably come at dusk," I say, "so I will fly to the crow colony in daylight and try to be back before they come."

"Do you even know where you're going?" Phil asks.

I don't.

"Then let me come with you," he says. "I know the way, and Fruggie did tell you not to go alone. We'll set off after breakfast." I know I should object, but I am overcome with such relief that I just nod and gulp hard at the lump in my beak.

"And make sure you eat!" he calls as he flies off. "You'll need all the fuel you can find for a journey like that."

Whilst Phil goes to find his slugs, I read my leaf letter. The river birds from our stretch of water are on their way. Merula explains that the river birds — a small flock of moorhens and coots — have taken positions along the water's edge as sentries. Their help against the magpies will be invaluable, but I have no time to hang around. Bird Boy comes into the garden carrying something. He walks solemnly down the path and over to my boat, for all the world looking as if he knows of my plight. Perhaps he's overheard something, or noticed how thin my feathers have become. Whatever it is, he knows. I stand my ground, and as we eyeball each other. I marvel at his bird sense. He silently sets down a small tub, then goes to his fort, from where he watches me breakfast like a king. Bird Boy has brought me mealworms! I can hardly believe it. He sets the small tub down carefully, then retreats to his fort where he watches me with those knowing eyes. As I peck at the wriggly treats, I feel strength flowing back into my wings. This boy understands more than any human should.

Fired up by my feast, I call to Merula the blackbird, who will have to deputise for me whilst I'm away. A wind is picking up, and I have to call loud to be heard above the rustling leaves, but the sky is bright and blue overhead. Merula appears from the bush behind Bird Boy's fort. She looks exhausted.

"Just been helping Parus with her defences - she's still a bit shaken from hitting the window, and keeps panicking that her nest isn't hidden well enough"

"Have you eaten?" I ask, my guilty stomach writhing with delicious mealworms.

"No time. Parus needs constant reassurance - keeps wanting to abandon the nest and start over somewhere else."

"Come on," I say, "we'll talk whilst you eat." There are a lot of insects who have been rendered homeless by *Gunman* digging around the new fountain, and Merula takes her peck whilst I sit on the cordyline tree and explain where Phil and I are going. Having tried to persuade me against the trip, Merula then tries to convince me to let her come along.

"Three is safer than two," she insists.

"Don't be a fool, Merula. You have work to do here," I say determinedly, though she has a point about the safety of numbers. "Phil and I will be fine."

Merula stabs at another worm before responding.

"Three is safer than two," she insists, then stands still as a statue before going in for another worm, stabbing viciously with her brown beak. Still, then stab, still, then stab, all the while continuing to object to my mission.

And then I remember my trump card.

"Anyway, Merula, I need you here. I want you to run the lookout with Starry. And somebody needs to talk to the river birds when they arrive. Plus, Parus will never manage without your support — she needs someone steady to keep her calm."

I am relieved when Merula agrees to stay. She has

lost more children to the magpie mafia than any other bird in Riverside Garden, and today she needs to stay and help protect the little ones who still have a chance. With Merula holding the fort, it is vital that Phil and I take flight as soon as possible if we are to have any chance of getting home by dusk.

The darkening skies look ready to empty their load, and I suddenly feel a chill that has nothing to do with the coming storm.

Today might be the last day I ever see Riverside Garden.

chapter fifteen

Alcedo the Kingfisher

Alcedo nests in a tunnel by the stream.
She digs a new one each year. I only saw it once.
— From Bird Boy's Notebook —

Phil appears by my side, having said his farewells.

"We should go," he says grimly. "The weather is closing in." And so we set off on our sad message mission, Phil first, me flapping furiously behind, ten beats to his five, in my efforts to keep up. We fly over our house, across the lane, and up to the school.

My wings ache from fighting the wind, and I'm

grateful when Phil signals for a landing. We stop to rest high on the school roof, alert to predators and even more alert to attacks from resident birds, for this is not our territory and we certainly would not be welcome if spotted.

A low-pitched *butt-butt-butt* from behind us has us in the air in seconds, and we turn to see Hula the bullfinch crash land onto the apex of the roof. "You nearly scared the tail feathers off me!" I shriek. "What are you doing here?"

"I've come to join you," says Hula breathlessly.

My heart sinks: the last thing we need is a passenger.

"I flew up to your garden to see how you are all getting on and Merula told me where you'd gone. She says that three birds are better than two, so here I am, the third bird!"

Before I can begin to tweet my objections, Phil

chips in.

"OK, Hula, but you'll have to keep up and do as you're told."

Hula the bullfinch swells his strong pink breast and nods his neckless head.

We take off into the unknown, three birds bound together by duty and fear.

The rain has stopped but the wind blows hard. As we head over the main road — already further afield than I have ever flown — I know that as much as the favourable wind is hastening our journey now, it will seriously impede our return if it keeps up like this.

Phil calls for a rest — even his strong wings are trembling from the effort — and we gratefully settle by the water. Our second break is in a tree by the creek, where we meet a kingfisher. Unusually (for kingfishers are solitary, shy creatures), this beautiful bird, whose name is Alcedo, is sociable and charming. He quickly reassures us that we are not intruding on anybody's territory but his own, for he lives in a hole in the sandy bank immediately below where we perch. He offers us food, but not being fish eaters, we hastily decline.

Hula is chattier than Phil and me, and I suspect is trying to extend our rest period. He begins to tell Alcedo about the magpies and about Fruggie's martyred mission to find the goshawks.

"But I know Fruggie," says Alcedo. "He came this way after he was rejected by his colony. Oh, the poor bird was in a shocking state. I took him to a safe bank where he could drink and bathe his wounds. I've often wondered what became of him."

"He lived on Fishery Lane for a while," I say gently, sensing the shock our news has caused to Alcedo, "and his bravery in setting off to the Cliveden Woods alone is astounding."

"I'm not surprised," says Alcedo. "That same bird

nearly got pecked to death by his own colony because of his courage."

"Because of his courage? What happened to him? I didn't dare ask when we met," I say. The story that Alcedo tells us even silences Hula.

"Fruggie wanted his crow family to be kinder to small birds like us," Alcedo says sadly. "They live in the woods behind the nature reserve. Last winter, when humans built houses on their fields, the crows had to find food somewhere else. Fruggie thought they should go to the farmland and eat dead animals. But Crook, their leader, had different ideas. He made them come closer to home and steal from tiny songbirds." Alcedo looks at us with sympathy. "All the little birds died."

I gasp, my feathers standing on end.

"Crook was mean and greedy. When Fruggie tried to stop him, Crook and the other crows turned on Fruggie."

I am mesmerised by the sad story and by Alcedo's beauty as he perches motionless on his branch.

"But why is he in such bad shape?" I ask.

"They tried to kill him," says Alcedo. "They have their own rules. If one crow breaks them, the other crows punish them. Sometimes... sometimes they even kill them."

"You should meet Sage," mumbles Hula, "you both know everything."

"So how will we be received if we fly into the colony?" asks Phil, glaring at Hula. "Crook sounds unlikely to care about poor Fruggie's fate and unlikely to give us a sympathetic audience either."

"He will attack you, and he will kill you," says Alcedo simply. And then he adds, "You absolutely must not go."

I feel so relieved I could almost sing, and I can barely believe my ears when Hula puffs himself up to his best size — something fierce flickering in his eyes — and says, in a choked voice,

"We HAVE to go. Rube made a promise, and songbirds always keeps their promises. And poor Fruggie is dying because he tried to save us songbirds." There is an awkward silence. It is the first time somebody has actually voiced their worst fears about Fruggie's fate. Up until now, we have been fooling ourselves, hoping to find him safe and well on our return. Alcedo's tragic tale explains so much about Fruggie's foolhardy mission to find the goshawks, it explains why he is so adamant that I should not visit the crow colony alone, and most of all, it explains why he wants the tale of his final selfless quest to get back to his colony.

"A promise is a promise, and we songbirds have a high code of honour," Hula continues. "We must bring news of Fruggie back to his colony as he has asked us to do." Hula has changed. Since the evening with the peacocks, he has grown in confidence and stature, and I feel proud — if terrified — to hear his brave and honourable speech. "Isn't that right, Rube? Phil?" We have no choice but to nod in agreement, humbled by the position Hula has taken, silenced by his new authority as the tables turn and it seems that Hula the bullfinch takes charge of our quest.

"Let me go," says Alcedo. "The crows have no gripe with me; we have different diets and different territories. I'm not pretending I like them, but we have co-existed in a civilised enough manner over the years. Let me give them Fruggie's news. You go back to your gardens and defend your territory against the magpies, and I will gladly take your message to the crows."

"But what if Crook attacks you too?" I protest.

"Then at least you'll be alive to defend your garden," Alcedo replies simply.

“At least let me come with you,” insists Hula. “Phil and Rube can return to protect their territories against the magpies. I have no family to protect — mine are all long lost to the magpies — let me stay with you, Alcedo, and accompany you on your journey.”

And so it is agreed. Alcedo and Hula — a more unlikely pair of birds you couldn’t hope to meet.

chapter sixteen

Gunman the Human

He doesn't have a nest.
He has a shed.
With tools. And traps.
— From Bird Boy's Notebook –

The flight home feels different now — not just because we are flying into the wind, but because we carry the weight of Fruggie's true story. Alcedo's and Hula's brave mission gives me hope, but as Riverside Garden comes into view, my heart pounds with new urgency.

We arrive by late afternoon, hours before the expected attack

Merula is waiting on the boat bow, brimming with

news.

"The magpies are all up by the lock," she says grimly.

"Is Fruggie back?" I ask.

Merula shakes her head. "Afraid not. Starry sent some starlings to check up the river. No sign of him, but they are quite sure the magpies will be with us by tomorrow."

At least there's a chance of some food and rest before the big battle.

"And Bird Boy and *Gunman* have been out all day with ladders and look…" Merula shrieks excitedly, pointing a wing towards the conifer trees.

At first, I can't see what she's talking about. And then I realise.

"Wire net," she says with delight. "Big enough for us to get in and out but too small for the magpies."

"Genius, sheer genius," I breathe. "*Gunman* did

this?"

Merula nods, hopping about in excitement. "*Gunman* and Bird Boy. *Gunman* up a ladder and Bird Boy was holding his book and shouting directions at his father."

I suddenly realise what he's been scribbling in that book of his.

"Nesting places!" I twitter. "He's noted down all our nesting places, and somehow persuaded his father to net them in. It's extraordinary."

He knows. Somehow, he knows

"Did he do mine?" warbles Phil, and flies off to check.

Merula nods. "And Parus and her family, Starry too!"

For the second time this weekend, *Gunman* could have blown me down with a feather.

"And Rube," Merula continues, barely containing

her excitement, "you'll never believe what happened while you were away. Constable Peck was spying around the garden, and *Gunman* came outside with a black box and — BANG! — nearly shocked my feathers clean off! Then I realised — that thing Pica told us was a gun is not a weapon at all. It's just a noise-maker, to frighten away the magpies!"

I feel my world tilt. "You mean…"

"*Gunman's* been protecting Grace and Alba all along," Merula chirps. "He was scaring magpies away from their nest."

We got it all wrong. He wasn't hunting. He was guarding.

I feel heat under my feathers. All this time… we misjudged him.

"We should have known. A man who saved little Parus would never harm Grace and Alba."

"It's Pica's fault. He made sure we only saw what he wanted us to see."

We ruffle our feathers, puffed with hope, and flutter up to safer heights. But just as we're about to settle, a tremor passes through me. The starlings are whistling a strange new call from the boathouse roof; the dogs are barking in the house, and the light is slipping fast.

Something feels... off.

It isn't until Merula flies off, and I hop down from the boat for a peck around the lawn, that I realise what it is.

Fruggie.

Hunched, ruffled and too, too still.

One side of his face is raw and weeping, the feathers matted where his eye used to be.

The other stares at me — not sharp, not bright, just dull and grey.

"Fruggie," I squeak, "when did you get back? Did you find them?"

He shakes his great black head very slowly from left

to right, but says nothing.

"Are you OK? Have you eaten?" I tweet nervously. Of course, he isn't OK, and I don't know how to help him.

I freeze.

My wings won't move.

The black feathers that once bristled with courage now droop like torn leaves.

I want to chirp comfort, but my beak only opens and closes.

I hum the opening bar of the May-Day anthem — the four descending notes every chick knows before it can fly — and feel my heartbeat steady.

I need to talk to Sage.

"Stay there," I blurt, immediately realising how daft that sounds. I flap once to steel myself, and hum the first three notes of the dawn chorus. A robin's breath of bravery. Then I rise.

"Fetch the sparrows," Sage says. "They'll know how best to help the poor creature."

We have a small community of house sparrows in Riverside Garden, and they nest under the roof tiles on the lane side of the house. I can still hear the dogs barking and scrabbling at the door as I fly over the house, calling urgently to the sparrows, a social, chatty group, who are the carers in our little community. They take food to the elderly birds in winter; they nurse injured birds, and they care for orphans. If you're out of sorts, there's nothing more comforting than the chirping and chattering attentions of our dear house sparrows.

I quickly explain Fruggie's plight to Passer, the head of the flock, and she immediately calls her nursing team together. Passer arrives with two other sparrows, carrying soft moss and spider silk for bandages.

Dusk descends as we set off back over the house. Around me, the sparrows murmur low snatches of melody — comfort songs they've used for fledglings and featherless chicks. Notes as old as the eaves they nest in.

I feel panicked at how vulnerable Fruggie will be to predators if we don't move him before nightfall. Then, from behind me, a strange sound fills the air — a croaking, cawing, rasping sound that gets louder and louder. Soon the noise envelops us, and its source becomes screamingly apparent as we fly within sight of the garden.

My wings still, and a single note escapes me — a pure, instinctive chirrup, like calling to the dark.

No answer comes.

Then I freeze in mid-air.

The lawn is black with birds.

chapter seventeen

Crows

Crows build strong nests with thick walls.
They come back year after year. One crow builds. Two guard.
— From Bird Boy's Notebook —

Crows. Everywhere. Crows on our fence, on our path, on the flagpole, the boathouse, the trellis. Crows in the trees and the bushes and the flower beds. There are so many crows on the lawn that not a blade of grass can be seen and there are even crows lined along the edge of Bird Boy's fort, despite his crouching, goggle-eyed presence behind them. There must be hundreds and hundreds of crows, a murder of the creatures, all cawing at the top of their voices. The din is deafening.

A lone female stands at the foot of the flagpole and inclines, very slightly, her magnificent head. The cawing stops and there is silence. We were too late — while I was fetching help, poor Fruggie had died. After a short while, the same female, who I now understand is standing beside Fruggie's lifeless body, raises her head and lets out a blood-curdling, agonising call that pierces the silence. Then there is a frantic flurry of feathers and every crow takes off in unison and flies away in all directions. For just a few seconds the sky is filled with their huge, black bodies and then they're gone, leaving Fruggie dead and alone at the bottom of the flagpole in Riverside Garden.

A lone sparrow sings — no words, no tune — just the sound of breath and being. And though Fruggie cannot hear it, it keeps the silence from breaking us.

When the stillness settles and the dusk is well behind us, Bird Boy emerges from his fort, tear-stained and shaky. Clutching his book, he runs up to the house and comes back very quickly with the *Gunman.* They look down at Fruggie's lifeless body, then walk back to the house. I'm paralysed with shock. Fruggie, the hero of the songbirds, is lying dead in our garden and I know not what to do. But Bird Boy does.

Bright lights flood the lawn and suddenly we're transformed back to daylight. The house doors open and *Gunman*, followed by his five children, walks down the path to Fruggie's corpse. The children rush about collecting leaves and twigs which they lay in a box that Bird Boy is holding. Gradually, the garden birds find their courage again and, encouraged by the bright lights, begin to emerge from their hiding places. I can see Phil in the eucalyptus, Cory and The Finsters on the potato vine, and Starry and his starlings up on the boathouse roof. Passer and her flock of sparrows are perched still and respectfully on top of the trellis, whilst Merula stands boldly on the garden table. Parus and her family flutter down to the buddlea and I stand my ground on the bow of my boat.

It seems that having witnessed a crow funeral, Bird Boy is about to give us our own opportunity to say goodbye to Fruggie. Whilst his father digs a hole in the earth by the boathouse, Bird Boy lovingly lifts Fruggie's limp body and lays it gently in the leaf-lined box. Bird Boy's brothers and sisters cover Fruggie's body with leaves and they close the lid.

I see Grace and Alba sitting defiantly on the fence, right beside where *Gunman* is digging, determined to pay their last respects to Fruggie. Bird Boy shows his father the book. *Gunman* looks at Grace and Alba with new understanding. When he nods gently towards them, Bird Boy's smile lights up the garden. Grace and Alba coo, and somehow we all understand that they are safe now.

After *Gunman* lowers Fruggie's box into the ground and covers it over with earth, Bird Boy pokes a bamboo cross into the soil and the family stands quietly, heads lowered, for a few moments. Then suddenly Phil bursts into song, joined quickly by Merula and The Finsters. Grace and Alba coo out their notes and Starry and the starlings sing beautifully from the boathouse roof. The Titchies, the sparrows and finally I, the proud lead singer of the choir, join in the final chorus for Fruggie, the hero of the songbirds.

Very much later that night I hear a rustle in the hedgerow and look to see *Gunman*, lit only by moon beams, climbing a long, wobbly ladder, wire netting clenched between his teeth, on his way up to protect Hope and Grace's nest from the magpies.

chapter eighteen

The Songbird Army

Some birds guard their nests. Some sing over them.
This time, they stand together.
— From Bird Boy's Notebook —

The magpies come the next morning at dawn. All night the rain has fallen — nature's tears for Fruggie — and now the garden drips with uncertainty. My feathers are damp, my heart racing. Are we ready for this?

Major, the great tit, brings the warning and bravely stays to join us for the battle.

"'Battle stations!' shrieks Starry from the boathouse

as hundreds of starlings appear as if from nowhere.

Major's sharp *tea-cher! tea-cher! tea-CHER*! cuts through the chaos like a battle drum: "Formation positions, Titchies!"

“Check supplies!” tweet the sparrows from the rooftop. And then, like a sunburst on a cloudy day, I hear a voice I recognise.

“Hula!” I shout through the chaos. “You’re back!” Hula looks stronger, fitter, more determined than before. He stands proud and firm on the bow of my boat, blinking slowly in the morning light.

“Alcedo too,” he points a wing towards the pontoon where Alcedo poses, dazzling and perfectly still, on a wooden post. He winks one eye in acknowledgement, and I curtsy my reply.

And then I hear the soft, deliberate clack of claws on wood. A hush spreads around the boat as a figure emerges slowly from the shadow of the mast —

unmistakable, dignified, and calm.

Sage.

Her green plumage has dulled with age, but her eyes are bright and full of fire. She walks carefully across the deck and settles beside Hula with a sigh, her claws curling into the worn wood of the prow. Her wings, clipped and useless for flight, hang motionless at her sides — but her presence is a steadying force.

She nods once towards me — not a greeting, exactly, but a sign that she's ready. She surveys our preparations with tactical eyes, then gives a barely perceptible signal to Hula. He immediately repositions The Finsters. Somehow, she's seen something we've missed.

The nesting birds have done the unthinkable — left their eggs and chicks — because today determines whether there will be any tomorrow. My wings tremble as I look from face to face — every parent in our community, here, trusting me with everything they have.

Suddenly, the air fills with the most magnificent shrieking I've ever heard — not angry like the magpies, but proud and fierce. Two enormous shapes come gliding over the garden fence, iridescent tail feathers streaming behind them like royal banners.

Petra and Perseus, the peacocks from three gardens up, land with surprising grace on either side of the lawn. "Did someone call for reinforcements?" Petra calls out, her voice regal even in battle mode.

"Not a moment too soon, it appears," tweets Hula. "Who's running The Finsters?"

"Cory the greenfinch," I say, "but she's too timid for a day like this."

"Then allow me," says Hula, and just as he is about to put out a call, he hears Major's cry.

"Battle stations!"

Chief Inspector Pica lands in the middle of our

lawn, flanked by Sergeant Pie and Constable Peck. The temperature drops, and I shrink into my plumage, but hold my position despite my racing heart. The huge magpies hop towards me, their cold, black eyes sweeping the hedges methodically. The entire garden falls deathly silent.

"We are here," he barks in his hoarse, unmusical voice, his gaze never stopping its calculating assessment, "to collect protection payment for the season in the usual manner." He pauses, head tilting as those predator eyes fix on the conifer hedge, weighing resistance. A couple of menacing bounds bring him closer, his sheer bulk making the ground seem to shudder. "This need not be a bloodbath if you stand back and let us take our dues." There is rustling and twittering from the camouflage of the bushes and trees. "But my forces will be here shortly, and make no mistake, payments will be made and scores will be settled." He hops around and looks at me standing defiantly on the bow of my boat. “Rube,” he says, “you know the score. It’s your responsibility to make sure this goes smoothly.”

"The only thing that's going smoothly, Pica," I call back, my voice steady despite my racing heart, "is your departure from Riverside Garden. This is our home, and you're not taking a single egg, a single chick, or even a single seed from this garden ever again."

"ATTACK!" shrieks Major from the top of the sycamore, but I raise a wing — not yet.

"Wait for my signal!" I shout. From my high perch, I can see Pica's reinforcements circling above, hesitant to land. "Starlings — NOW!" Group one erupts with their cat calls while I direct the battle like a conductor.

"Hula — show them the slingshots! Parus, Finsters to the bird bath!"

I can hardly believe my eyes when Parus and her cousin shoot out of the tree, each holding one end of a red rubber band.

Hula swoops down, grabs the rubber band's centre with his beak, loads a twig with his feet, and releases. “Like this!” The stick arrows towards Pica, piercing the lawn behind him.

The Finsters burst into a bright, defiant tink-tink-tink-tink! — a rapid-fire chorus that sounds like tiny war bells as they take their positions. Hula leads them to the upper tiers of the new bird bath, its multiple levels giving them perfect slingshot positions while the water below creates a confusing maze of reflections that makes it impossible for Pica to track the darting movements of his smaller opponents.

The stick flies like an arrow and pierces the lawn behind Pica. He hops about and barks angrily, and the conifer hedge erupts with similar teams of Titchies and Finsters slinging their sticks and stones to break the bones of the magpie they loathe so much.

A cat yowls behind me, then another in the corner, then another on the roof, and another under the fort.

“MMMEEEAAAAOOOWW!” they yell. “MMEEEAAAOOWW!” The garden is full of cat calls from Starry's starlings — perfect mimicry of the magpies' greatest fear. “MMEEEAAAAOOOOW!”

Between the yowling, Starry’s sharp whistle pierces the air — three short blasts that coordinate his squads like a general’s horn.

The yowling ruffles Pica, who calls for reinforcements. Sergeant Pie swoops down first, followed by two more black and whites, but the others hover and perch above the lawn, unsure about the cat calls from the hidden corners of the garden.

"More magpies incoming from the east!" I shout from my lookout post. "Starlings group two — get ready!"

While Pica screeches at them to land, a grinding,

irascible *gra-gra-gra-gra* noise comes from above. There is a familiar cawing din, and multitudes of crows descend on our garden for the second time in two days. I have no more than a moment to wonder why they have returned before the female who led Fruggie's mourning emits a blood-chilling war cry, and the crows mob those airborne magpies who have been too cowardly to land for fear of the feline yowling of Starry and his starlings.

Constable Peck shrieks orders, but her voice is lost in the chaos.

Sage shifts her stance slightly. She does not speak, but gives one short nod. Hula sees it. So do I.

It's the cue we didn't know we were waiting for — the signal to escalate.

The garden trembles with momentum.

chapter twenty

The Goshawks!

Goshawks nest in the deep woods.
They use the same nest for years.
It gets bigger and bigger..
So do they.
— From Bird Boy's Notebook —

Beneath the vicious, bloody battle between the crows and the magpies, I spot Pica trying to slip away towards the boathouse.

"He's escaping!" I cry, my voice breaking into the robin's ancient war cry — *tic-tic-tic-tic* — sharp as breaking twigs. "Phil, Merula — with me!"

We dive on Pica as he attempts to hop quietly from

the scene. Six tiny feet scrabble, six little wings beat, and three minute beaks peck at him. But they are no match for the mighty Pica, who swats us away.

“Backup please!” Phil's voice booms across the garden — a fierce rattling cry that makes the air tremble.

Grace and Alba respond immediately, swooping from their home to join the fight. A whoosh from above — nine Canada geese zoom over our heads, flying in a perfect diamond formation.

"Geese!" I shout, "He's by the boathouse wall — come in low on the next pass!"

They turn, then return, flying lower and faster so that we garden birds have to flatten ourselves to the ground to avoid being hit. Pica flaps his wings and barks angrily as the geese turn for the final flyby that I pray will beat him, but as they make their turn, Pica manages to hop to the base of the boathouse, too close to the building for the geese to make contact. They fly over, then land with a tremendous splash in the river at the end of the garden, bobbing about, waiting for their next chance.

Magpies are evil birds. They relish a battle. Pica shouts with glee from his cowardly shelter, and I feel a moment of despair — have I led everyone into disaster? But then I remember why we're fighting.

For Fruggie.

For every chick that will hatch this spring.

For the right to call this garden home.

"Starlings group three!" I call out, my voice stronger than ever. "Time for the mimicry!"

From their hidden positions, I hear Starry's specially trained squad begin their deception. In perfect imitation of Pica's harsh voice, they call out: "Stand down immediately!" "Return to base — urgent orders!" "Mission aborted!"

The confusion is instant — several magpies halt

mid-flight, wheeling around uncertainly, unsure whether the commands are real. Even Pica's head snaps up, scanning the sky for the source of what sounds like his own voice giving contradictory orders.

Then the house door opens, and Starlings group two shoots into action, flying to the end of the garden and emitting an extraordinary high-pitched whistle to drive the dogs to distraction. The huge wrinkly house dog and the little yappy one thunder down the garden, all barks blazing, and Starry's superbly trained squad swoops and circles tantalisingly out of reach while the dogs pelt around the garden after them. Starlings group one is still yowling their cat calls, group two is whistling their dog taunts, group three continues their magpie mimicry, and pretty soon I think that every dog in the neighbourhood is barking!

The crows caw and croak, the little songbirds shriek their warning calls — so much din that nobody hears

Bird Boy slip out of the house.

He comes silently down the path, holding a black box in outstretched arms. His eyes scan the garden, like he's trying to decode the chaos.

Then he sets the bird scarer down and triggers it.

Crack-crack-crack!

The sharp bangs echo across the garden, and the lawn falls quiet, scattered with feathers and sticks, but not a bird in sight.

Then Chief Inspector Pica emerges from under the boathouse and swaggers across the grass. His evil black eyes lock onto me as he addresses the hidden songbirds in a defiant snarl.

"We will be back," he growls, "but first, I'll deal with you personally, little robin."

He lurches towards me, his massive black and white body looms over me — I'm no bigger than his foot. As he gets closer, the stench of his breath — rotten eggs and dead things — makes me gag. His cruel beak snaps inches from my face.

My heart hammers against my ribcage. Every instinct screams at me to fly, hide, run.

But I think of Fruggie.

I think of every chick that will hatch this spring.

My talons grip the grass, and somehow I hold my ground.

"You're not welcome here," I whisper, my voice barely audible but steady. "Not today, not ever."

Pica throws back his head and cackles, his foul breath washing over me. He raises one massive wing, ready to strike.

And as he prepares to strike, a sharp, piercing *kek-kek-kek*! cuts through the silence.

I hop back, my whole body trembling. Every other bird in the garden freezes in terror.

And then, in the space of a heartbeat, comes the

impossible: a huge raptor swoops, grabs Chief Inspector Pica with its massive, outstretched talons, and in a few relaxed wing beats, flies up and off into the cold blue sky.

As Pica flaps and twitches in its grip, the enormous goshawk flies across the river and effortlessly back up above the treetops to join its mate, and the two magnificent creatures glide elegantly downstream back to their home in the Cliveden Woods.

The garden seems to breath, and a shaft of sunlight catches on the bow of my boat, where Sage stands with quiet dignity. She lowers her head in a deep, dignified nod.

And the Songbird Choir bursts into song.

epilogue

From Bird Boy's Notebook

A little bird told me…

Chief Inspector Pica

Vanished without a trace. No one dares speak his name — not even the crows.

Sergeant Pie

Also gone. The garden is quieter now.

Crook

Overthrown by his own colony. The female who led Fruggie's farewell took over, and things have been better since.

Grace and Alba

Moved to my balcony. I feed them every morning. They wait

for me now.

Hula

Took charge of The Finsters. Rules with heart, not just feathers.

Major

Partners with Hula. Keeps the peace. Still shouts sometimes. His two are thriving.

Cory the Greenfinch

Writes poems. Quiet poems. Her clutch hatched safely — courage found its reward.

Merula

Still the first voice I hear in the morning. Built again after the victory — five eggs, five survivors.

Phil

Still around. I think he knows more than he lets on. His four chicks fledged just in time — all safe.

Parus

Hasn't hit a window since. Sees things clearly now. Her

rushed nest worked — three healthy fledglings.

Rube

Ran the Songbird Choir till the very end. The garden felt different after his last note. Sometimes I wonder if Rube would approve of how I told his story.

Starry

Runs the Spring Singing Contest. Wins every time. Still insists it's fair.

Some mornings, if I sit very still while I write my stories, I hear the songbirds chorus my name.

About the Author

Hi, I'm Julia, a children's author with a big love for birds, bugs, and all things wild. I grew up on a farm in Somerset and have been scribbling nature-inspired stories ever since my five children were small enough to dig for worms in the garden.

I believe that nature is full of hidden adventures — if you only stop to look. My books invite readers to step into those worlds, where dragonflies shimmer with secrets, songbirds band together to fight battles of courage and hope, and even the smallest creatures can make a big difference.

I'm the author of **The Songbird Army** and **The Lost Dragonflies**, stories full of feathery friends, magical discoveries, and thrilling adventures in the natural world. I write alongside my trusty bull terrier, **Muttley**, who likes reading over my shoulder when she's not chasing birds around the garden.

If you enjoyed this story, I'd love it if you left a review on **Amazon** — or you can get in touch through my website, where you can find fun wildlife facts, quizzes, and sneak peeks of my next books:

JuliaBlackburn.co.uk

* * *

Printed in Dunstable, United Kingdom

71187351R00099